HAWAIIAN SHAPESHIFTER II

DOLPHINS & HUMANS

D J Wallace

Ellen Wallace

Hawaiian Shapeshifter II

Dolphins & Humans

D J Wallace

Ellen Wallace

Disclaimer

Contents

NOTE TO READER..4

Hawaiian Shapeshifters of Legend.......................4

Chapter 1: Leila & Misty....................................7

Chapter 2: A Safe Place to Heal........................19

Chapter 3: The Puhi Cave.................................31

Chapter 4: Mending Wounds.............................43

About The Author...71

OTHER BOOKS BY DJ WALLACE ON AMAZON 72

TAROT READING..73

NOTE TO READER

Dolphins, Eels & Humans is taken from my Kindle Vella Series, *The Shark Man of Haleiwa.* Since Kindle Vella is only available in the United States, I am reprinting these stories in book form to reach a broader audience. The stories have been slightly altered to fit the book format.

Hawaiian Shapeshifters of Legend

Hawaiian legends speak of shapeshifters known as Kupua. Kupua were demigods that could transform into animals or other natural forms such as water, trees, or clouds. A famous Kupua mentioned by Hawaiians is Kamapua'a.

As a demigod, Kamapua'a was half man and half pig. He is remembered for his epic battles and love affairs with Pele, the goddess of fire. Kamapua'a's home is found in Nu'uanu on the island of Oahu. He is credited with creating the deep grooves in the Ko'olau mountain range using his large sharp tusks.

Hawaiians also have a belief in Aumakua, family guardians. Aumakua were deceased family members who agreed to serve as protectors for the family. The Aumakua appeared to family members in a form that was recognized by the family. Aumakua will have a name and can occur as a specific shark, eel, owl, or other form. Just because your Aumakua appears to you as a shark does not mean all sharks are your Aumakua.

Hawaiian Shapeshifters #2 *Dolphins, Eels & Humans* is a fictional account that blends the Kupua and Aumakua traditions and examines the possibilities of Kupua and Aumakua surviving in the modern world. This series is centered around a family of shapeshifting eels and their rivalry with a family of shapeshifting sharks. Through their conflicts, you will be introduced to the shapeshifting underground of alliances, betrayal, love, and heroism, that connects our rivals to other shape-shifting families.

PROLOGUE

In book #1 *A Man Eater Is Born,* you were introduced to Aunty Momi who had adopted several shape shifters which include a dolphin, frigate bird, owl, and a baby shark. Aunty Momi and her two sons, Martin, and Paul, are shape shifting eels.

When Aunty Momi takes the baby shark to the ocean for the first time, Leila, the shape shifting dolphin, decides to search for her mother Misty. What Leila finds changes her life forever.

Chapter 1: Leila & Misty

By the time Leila finally found her mother, it was late in the evening when Spinner dolphins usually hunt in deeper water.

Leila could sense something terrible had happened as she homed in on her mom's Misty signals. Instead of finding a large pod of other dolphins as was the norm, she could only identify four individual dolphins tightly packed together. Finally, she spotted four dolphins and noticed that Misty was injured and swimming slowly.

"Momma!" called Leila. "What happened to you?"

"Your momma tried to protect her baby Nalu," said Thunder, one of the pod's male protectors.

"Blacktip sharks attacked Nalu while we were resting before the evening hunt."

"I pushed Nalu out of the way," said a gasping Misty, "but one shark grabbed my tail, and bit down on it. In the struggle, I lost most of my tail. Without my tail, I can't keep up with the rest of the pod."

"Don't worry, Momma," said Misty's older son, Streak. "We will take care of you."

Leila swam to the back of Misty to inspect the damage to her tail. Horror overcame her. Only a tiny piece of the right side of her tail remained, leaving part of her tailbone exposed. While the salt water kept the wound clean, the exposed flesh was an open invitation to hungry sharks.

"Where's the rest of the family?" asked Leila.

"They are hunting right now," said Thunder. "We take turns watching Momma, and the hunters bring back enough food for us to share. We take care of our own."

The Mokuleia pod Leila was born into was a network of several smaller pods that freely intermingled with each other. Misty led her family group: her four sisters, their five children, and two large males.

"The hunters are returning," clicked Thunder. "Perfect timing. My stomach is burning a hole."

Leila and Streak raced out to greet the hunters, hoping to snag some food for their mother. Each of the returning hunters had their beaks filled with shrimp, squid, and lantern fish and willingly surrendered their catch to Leila and Streak.

"Thank you, Aunty," whistled Leila.

"You are welcome, Lei," replied Rose, Misty's oldest sister. "Welcome home. You came at a good time. Your mom needs your help."

"Yes, Aunty, I saw her injuries. Is there anything we can do to help Momma?"

"Not really," answered Rose, "unless you know someone who can regrow your momma a new tail."

Leila nodded and darted back to Misty with all the fish she could stuff into her beak. Misty quickly swallowed Leila's offerings, followed by more food from the returning hunters.

Eating her fill, Misty relaxed and placed her left pectoral fin on Leila to gain some buoyancy.

"It's been a while since you visited us, Leila," said Misty. "What is going on with you?"

"I want to thank you for letting me stay with the Puhi family. I am enjoying my adopted brothers and sisters very much. I appreciate the human world the longer I am with Aunty Momi and Uncle Victor. At least I don't have to worry about being eaten alive by sharks."

"Trust me, there are far worse things than sharks on land. Humans can be cruel and blood thirsty. Sharks kill for food. Humans do it for sport. Just like the idiot who shot you."

"All the humans I met, in Haleiwa and school are not like that, Momma."

"Then I am glad that Aunty Momi and Uncle Victor have kept you away from that."

"Momma, I love you and my family, but I know I am different from everyone else in the family."

"You are referring to your human side. Is that right?"

"Yes, I am, Momma. I need to find out where I belong. Am I the only one like this in the family? And who is my dad? I have so many questions."

Misty grinned. "First, you are not the only family member who can change forms. Aunty Rose and I are shapeshifters, too."

"I suspected you might be, but not Aunty Rose."

"Aunty Rose had too many run-ins with humans. She despises them, but for me, it was very different."

"What do you mean, Momma?"

"Well, a fisherman used to lay his net just outside the breakers in Waialua. I was curious about him, so I swam to his boat one day to get a better look at him. When I saw him, I couldn't take my eyes off him. He was the most magnificent creature I ever saw on land or in the ocean."

Leila smiled, sensing where the story was heading. "And what happened?"

"When I popped out of the water in my dolphin form, the man smiled and said "hello." Since I didn't swim away, he reached over the side of his boat and rubbed my head in its most sensitive spot. It sent electricity through my body, and before I knew it, I was in love."

Leila laughed. "Mom, you are so easy! Tell me more!"

"The man set his net, then asked if I could help him catch fish. He did not know I understood everything he said to me. I sped away from his boat, found a small school of rabbitfish, and herded them into his net. The net was so full that he had difficulty pulling it onto his boat. He was happy with his catch and shared some fish with me, always rubbing my sensitive spot while he fed me."

"So, whatever happened between you and this human?"

"I continued to help fill his net with fish every time I saw his boat in the bay, and he trusted me more and more. Then, one day, he told me something I never thought I would hear."

"What was that, Momma?"

"He said he wished I was a woman so he could take me home with him."

"Wow."

"Yeah. I wanted to be with this man so much that my body ached. I knew I was a woman and could be with him in my human form when I shifted. To be with him, I needed a plan."

"What did you do, Momma?"

"One day, when the man set his net, I purposely swam into his net and allowed myself to get tangled in it. He pulled me onto his boat to free me. Once on his boat, I shifted into my human form."

Mesmerized by her mother's story, Leila asked, "How did the man react to you in your human form?"

"At first, I startled him. He backed away to the edge of his boat and stared at me for a long time. I knew he was confused. He then realized I was naked, so he gave me his yellow rain jacket to cover myself."

"Did he say anything to you?"

"Not right away. It took him a while to accept what he witnessed and to realize he wasn't delusional. After several minutes of stunned silence, he finally smiled and spoke."

"Hi, I'm Chris," and he extended his hand. "You're the ah."

"The dolphin?" Misty nodded. "I am called Misty."

"I grabbed Chris' hand," continued Misty, "and pulled him down to me."

"Don't tell me you did it right there on the boat."

"Oh yes, baby girl. After all, I thought that would be the only time I would be with Chris, so I wanted to ensure I had my fill of him."

"Did it end up working out that way, Mom?"

Misty laughed. "No, it didn't. Chris was such a sweet, tender lover that I spent the next six months on land, living as a woman in Chris' home. I met his parents, friends, and siblings. Then I found out I was pregnant."

"You got pregnant from a human? How did the child turn out?"

"This is how we pass the shapeshifting ability to the next generation. We female dolphins who have the shapeshifting genes in us must mate with a human. Besides, I think the child from this mating is doing very well, aren't you?"

"What? This is me you are talking about? My dad is a fisherman named Chris?"

"Yes, that is correct. I meant to take you to him, but I'm not sure it is a good idea now."

"You think your missing tail and feet will change his feelings for you?"

"No, this has nothing to do with my feet. It's been over ten years since I left Chris without explaining why, so I don't know how he will react. He could have a human family by now. I don't want to interfere with his life and cause trouble for him if he has a wife and children."

Leila paused in thought as she absorbed what Misty had divulged. Finally, she said, "Mom, let's deal with your wounds before deciding about Chris. It would be best to heal in a better place than the open ocean, where predators can attack you. Momi and her family use a cove to heal themselves. The ancestral eels of the bay know the different remedies to heal anything, and I am sure they would be happy to help you."

"Healing the wounds is one thing, but how can I grow back my tail fins to swim better? Do they have a miracle to do that?"

Leila smiled. "Uncle Victor is the miracle worker. He's a licensed engineer but a fisherman by choice. You should see the things he created for fishing. The man is way ahead of his time. I am sure he can make something to help you swim better."

By this time, the entire pod had returned from hunting and gathered around Leila and Misty, listening intently to what was being discussed.

"Sister," said Anna, Misty's older sister. "I agree with Leila. The eels are famous for their miracle cures, so you should use their skills. You will be safer in the cove than in the open sea."

"Yes, Anna," replied Leila. "My land mother, Aunty Momi, is family to the eels there, and she will make sure Momma is safe."

"But what about me?" asked Nalu, upset that he would be separated from his mother Misty. "Who's going to take care of me?"

"We will take care of you, since your Momma can't take care of herself right now," said Anna. "The cave with the eels is your Momma's best chance of healing in safety."

"Yes, little brother," said Streak. "We got you. That is what family is all about."

"Besides," added Leila, "we will still be near the ocean, and you can visit Momma any time you want."

Misty stroked little Nalu to soothe his worries. "You will be fine, son. Don't worry. I will be back to the pod as soon as I can."

"You promise?" asked Nalu.

"Yes," nodded Misty. "I promise."

Seeing that all worries were resolved, Misty addressed the pod.

"At first light, Leila and Thunder will help me to the eel cove. While I am gone, Sister Anna will be the pod leader. She has navigated these grounds for as long as I have, so she will keep you fed and safe. Meanwhile, let's rest and prepare for the journey to shore."

The pod clustered close together and shut down half of their brains. They were in survival mode, gliding through the water while surfacing periodically to breathe. Since Leila had spent too much time away from the pod, she had difficulty resting half her brain. Being fully alert while the rest of the pod slept reminded Leila of how different she was from the rest of her family.

At the Puhi homestead, Momi had a restless night caring for Fins and worrying about Leila. Now that Fins had assumed his human form, he was up every two hours demanding a milk bottle. Since Fins had eaten solid food, his poop was rancid, and the stench fouled the air in Momi and Victor's bedroom.

"Wow," exclaimed Victor as he changed Fin's diaper. "I never knew digested human flesh smelled this bad. My nose and eyeballs are ready to pop!"

"At least we don't have to deal with those teeth," replied Momi as she opened the bedroom windows and door wider to let in the trade winds.

"I agree." Victor finished cleaning Fins and refitted him with a new diaper. Fins smiled in his approval as Momi picked him up and gave him a fresh bottle.

"So, what will you do about Leila?" asked Victor.

"At first light, I am taking Hoku, and we are going to Kaena to see if we can spot her. We need to find out what happened to her mom and decide if we can help her."

"Sounds good. I'll stay with Fins. Tina and Maile can help me with the rest of the kids. There's no school tomorrow, and I only have one charter in the late afternoon. We should be fine."

A few minutes after emptying his bottle and letting out an enormous burp, Fins fell into a deep sleep, prompting Momi and Victor to follow suit.

Hoku was the alarm clock for the Puhi family. The rising sun triggered Hoku's shapeshifting, which was irresistible and instinctual. Every morning moments before dawn, Hoku disrobed and stood naked in the secluded backyard as she quickly shifted into a giant frigate bird. Her long black feathers that itched beneath her human skin emerged like a garden of blooming flowers. Flying to the top of a 10-foot pole and crosspiece Victor had built for her, Hoku could stretch her 8-foot wingspan and test the morning breeze. As the sun's warmth filled the morning air, Hoku flapped her wings to energize her mind and body. When the sun cleared the horizon, Hoku returned to the ground and assumed her human form, feeling refreshed and rejuvenated. As Hoku grew older, she learned to keep her feathers to cover her private parts. The feather cover made it appear that Hoku was wearing a one-piece bathing suit.

Momi had seen Hoku's morning rituals many times but was still in awe each time. This morning, however, there was a sense of urgency in Momi's voice.

"Hoku," called Momi from the back porch, "I need your help with Leila today. Can you help me find her? They should be closer to shore now that the sun is rising."

"Sure, Aunty, that should be easy."

"I was hoping you'd say that. Come inside, get something to eat, and let's head out to Kaena. Something is wrong. Leila's in trouble. We need to find her. She needs our help."

Chapter 2: A Safe Place to Heal

After a long night of hunting and feasting, the rising sun was a welcome sight for Leila, Thunder, and Misty. Misty was exhausted from using only her pectoral flippers to swim and prevented her from hunting with the rest of the family. The best she could do was follow in the wake of the hunters and depend on their generosity for her meal. The hunters were mindful of Misty, Leila, and Thunder and made several trips to them with beaks filled with squid and fish. Leila and Thunder guarded Misty from the sharks that were active during the night. Fortunately, the waters between Oahu and Kauai, where the pod fed, teamed with fish and squid, providing dolphins and sharks with easy prey. Still, guarding Misty required Leila's and Thunder's complete attention, which was mentally and emotionally draining.

As the hunt waned, the pod members began to cluster around Misty, bringing instant relief to Leila and Thunder.

"Finally!" clicked Leila. "I thought the daylight would never get here!"

"Sorry for keeping you from the hunt," clicked Misty. "But thanks for keeping an eye out for me. Hopefully, I can find a new way to swim without my tail."

"It has been done," added Thunder. "I know you can do it too."

"Thanks, Thunder," said Misty. "It will take a lot of work, but I know I can do this."

The pod moved closer to shore and began shutting half of its brain in preparation for sleeping.

****

Hoku soared high above the waves in her frigate bird form, searching for Leila. Several small pods of dolphins gathered near Ka'ena Point, so finding Leila's pod proved tricky. Finally, as Hoku circled a pod just outside Mokuleia, she saw a dolphin leap into the air.

"Hoku!" called Leila. "Is that you?" Spotting Hoku in a sky filled with other frigate birds was easy for Leila. Hoku was the largest frigate bird in the sky.

Hoku banked to her left and answered. "Leila! Yes! It's me, Hoku." Hoku glided down closer to the water's surface and hovered over Leila.

"Aunty Momi asked me to look for you," said Hoku. "She is waiting for me at the cove. What is happening with your mom?"

"Thanks for finding us," replied Leila. "My mom lost her tail when a shark bit her, and now the rest of the family is caring for her."

"That is unfortunate," replied Hoku.

"Is she okay?

"She is struggling to keep up with the rest of the pod, but they are taking good care of her. She needs a safe place to heal, though. Trying to stay with the pod without her tail is exhausting for her."

What do you want me to tell Aunty Momi?" asked Hoku.

"I want to ask Aunty if I could take my mom to the cove and have the eels in the bay help her heal. Can you check with Aunty to see if it is okay to take her there?"

"Sure, I will do that right now. Be right back."

"Thanks, Hoku!"

Hoku turned to the wind and shot high into the sky, then coasted easily to Eel Cove, where Momi anxiously awaited.

"Aunty," said Hoku as she landed and shifted to her feathery human form. "I found Leila and her mother. They are just outside the breakers at Mokuleia, moving toward Kaena."

"Thank you, Hoku," said Momi. "What's going on?"

"A shark attacked Leila's mom and bit off her tail. From what I could see, the wound is still raw, and her mom is struggling to keep up with her pod."

"Wow. Losing a tail is serious. That's how they get their power to swim. That makes it hard for her to hunt and escape sharks."

"Leila asked if she could take her mom to Eel Cove and have the ancestors help her heal."

"That sounds like an excellent idea. Hoku, return to Leila and tell her to bring her mom here. I will ask the ancestors if that is okay. I am sure it will not be a problem."

Hoku sprinted into the wind and shifted into a frigate bird. She flew into the morning sky, searching once again for Leila and her family. She found them just outside the Polo field and dove toward the pod.

"Leila," called Hoku, "Aunty said to take your mom to the cove. She's waiting for you there."

"What's going on with you and that black bird?" asked Misty.

"The bird is my friend Hoku. She is a shapeshifter like us but turns into that frigate bird. She lives with the family that takes care of me. Hoku says we can take you to Eel Cove, where the eels will help you heal. Remember what we talked about last night?"

"Oh yes, the eel cove, a safe place for me to heal."

"Let me show you the way, Mom."

Leila gently led Misty to Eel Cove while the entire pod, still in their sleeping mode, followed them. When Leila and Misty reached the mouth of the cove, they paused in the water and popped their human heads above the surface. Leila turned to Thunder and said, "I'll take it from here. The rest of the family can go now." Thunder slapped the water with his tail and hurried away from the cove, followed by the rest of the family.

On shore, Hoku solemnly stood next to Momi, who chanted, asking the ancestors' permission for Leila and her mother to enter the sacred grounds. Long, dark, tubular shadows emerged from the cove and swarmed around Leila and Misty. A friendly voice echoed from the deep. "Welcome home, Leila. You and your mother are welcome here. Enter so we may embrace you."

"Thank you, ancestors, Aunty Momi," answered Leila. "This is my mother, Misty. She needs your help."

"Yes," said the voice, "We see that. It is a nasty wound. We can help heal the wound, but we do not have the magic to regrow a tail."

"That's okay, ancestor," said Leila, "We need to take care of the wound first; then maybe Uncle Victor can help with the tail."

"That would be a good challenge for Uncle Victor," said Momi. "He can put his skills to the test. It would be good if Uncle worked on getting your mom a tail and feet since she is a shapeshifter."

"Oh, a tail would be good," said Misty. "I rarely come on land anymore. I think I forgot to be a human and walk on two legs."

"Swim into this small tidal pool so I can see how the shark bite affected your human parts. Hoku, run to the truck and get me a beach towel to cover Misty. Grab another one for Leila. May as well you get dressed too, Hoku."

Leila and Misty emerged from the ocean and entered the tidal pool as directed by Momi. As the two female dolphins morphed into their human form, they looked more like sisters than mother and daughter. Their dark brown hair flowed down the back of their backs, and their bodies glistened with a golden glow. Their faces looked as though a master carver sculpted them. They were stunning. Spending time in the ocean helped accentuate Leila's incredible human features.

"Let me see your feet," asked Momi.

Misty pulled up both of her legs, revealing the ghastly injury. Both of Misty's feet were severed below the ankle. Bone, muscles, and tendons were exposed, making Aunty Momi nauseous.

"That is nasty," gagged Leila.

"Ancestor," asked Aunty Momi, "Can you heal this injury?"

"Yes, we can," replied the Ancestor. "We have seen this type of injury before. Treating Misty as a dolphin rather than a human would be best until the wound heals."

"Yes, that would be easier," agreed Momi. "After we solve the dolphin problem, we can solve the human problem."

"How long will this take?" asked Misty.

"As long as it needs," answered Ancestor. "We will protect you, feed you, and help you heal as long as necessary."

"I'll come down and visit with you every day, Mom," added Leila.

"My husband Victor and I will help settle you in the bay," said Aunty Momi. "We can bring you clothes and anything else you need to get you accustomed to human life on land."

"Wahinepuhi," said the Ancestor. "Since this place is busy with people during the day when Misty would be sleeping, we must keep her safe."

"You want me to take her to the cave?" asked Aunty Momi. "Are you sure about that?"

"Yes," replied the Ancestor. "Take her to the cave."

"Aunty," asked Leila. "What cave are you talking about?"

"It's the place where the bones of my ancestors are hidden," answered Aunty Momi. "This bay is a gateway to that place."

"Can I come along with you and Mom?" asked Leila.

"How about me, too?" asked Hoku.

"You are ohana," answered the Ancestor. "Yes, both of you may come. Remember, the cave's location should not be revealed to anyone outside the family. Come, let's go."

A thick, dark, tubular shadow appeared in the bay beyond the shore. It paused briefly, waiting for the others to join it. Aunty Momi entered the bay and transformed into a giant spotted Moray eel. Turning to Hoku, Aunty Momi said, "Come on, jump on my back and hold on."

Hoku leaped onto Aunty Momi's back and placed a stranglehold on Aunty Momi's eel form. Leila and Misty returned to the cove and shifted to their dolphin forms.

Upon entering the ocean, Leila and Misty were shocked to see the largest Moray eel they had ever seen. It looked more like a mini submarine than an eel. The eel cruised through the water, unafraid and in total command. This was the Ancestor, the eel behind the voice speaking to them.

The Ancestor led the group to a large outcropping of black volcanic stone near the leaping spot in the bay. The volcanic boulders created a maze that led inland beneath the sandstone shoreline. At the end of the labyrinth was a narrow tunnel the Ancestor could barely squeeze through. The tunnel then opened to a large cavern of about 400 square feet.

As Aunty Momi, Hoku, Leila, and Misty surfaced in the cave, they were overwhelmed by what they saw. The reflected sunlight from the ocean lit the cave with an eerie greenish-blue hue, making everything glisten with energy. Ki'ai, or woven baskets that contained ancestors' bones lined the cave's walls and were stacked like bricks to the top of the cave. Some ki'ai were for human forms, while others were for the eel form. Several aged koa spears and feather cloaks were carefully displayed, along with a canoe, fishing nets, and fishhooks. A massive stone altar contained several bowls where food and 'awa were left to feed the ancestors.

"This is Hale Puhi," said the Ancestor as she emerged from the water and sat at the cavern's ledge. Ancestor then morphed into her human form, a kind grandmother with long white hair. "Come, come, sit with me," Ancestor insisted.

"Mahalo, ancestor," said Aunty Momi as she slid out of the water and sat beside Ancestor.

"Come, honi me," said Ancestor.

"Oh yes, Tutu," replied Momi as she pressed her nose against Ancestor and inhaled her ha energy.

"Hoku, Leila, Misty, show Tutu some love," said Momi.

After honi were exchanged, Ancestor addressed Misty.

"This is where you should spend your days. While you are here, we will have the cleaner fishes remove the dead flesh and skin from your wound so healing can take place. You must stick your leg or tail in the water, and the cleaner fish will care for you. We will treat the wound with different types of seaweed and herbs when they are done. Many of our family members were famous healers during their time, and they are all here to help you now."

"This place is kinda spooky," whispered Misty under her breath.

"And you think what humans would do to a tailless dolphin isn't spooky?" asked Ancestor.

Misty nodded, embarrassed that Ancestor heard her remark.

"I get your point. I just need to get used to this place. Please excuse my rude remark."

"I am not offended that you spoke your mind," Ancestor replied.

"Now, if you get lonely, there's lots of family you can talk to right here," said Ancestor.

"That's the problem," replied Misty. "Everyone in this cave except for us is dead."

Ancestor laughed. "Misty, you don't seem to have a problem with me. Right?"

"Oh no," smiled Misty. "I have no problem with you at all."

"Do you realize I have been dead for almost four hundred years?"

"Four hundred years!" gasped Misty and Leila.

"Yes, my human form is dead, but my spirit never dies." added Ancestor, "I am still me. Everyone here in this cavern is the same as me. We are not here to scare you or drive you insane. We are here to help you. Can you handle that?"

Misty nodded. "Sure, Ancestor. I can handle this. When do we start?"

"For you, the healing starts today. For Wahinepuhi, there is something they need to do."

"What is it?" asked Momi.

The Ancestor nodded toward the stone altar with several empty bowls on it. "You see that? They are empty, and we are hungry and thirsty. We would appreciate it if you could get us some of your Hiwa' awa, kai taro, poi, kalua pig, roasted chicken, dried aku, sweet potatoes, and breadfruit."

"Say no more," assured Momi. "Give me and the family a couple of days, and we will prepare a feast for you and the family."

"Oh, mahalo, my girl!" cried Ancestor. "Thank you so much. Don't worry about your friend. We will take good care of her."

Chapter 3: The Puhi Cave

The Ancestor faded from sight, leaving Misty, Momi, Hoku, and Leila alone in the cave, huddled together on a rocky ledge near an old canoe. Since they were outside of the ocean, they transformed into their human forms.

"Aunty, what are we going to do now?" asked Leila.

Momi smiled. "I know you may feel overwhelmed by what you see here, the bones of my ancestors stacked like pancakes on each other and all these ancient relics from a very colorful past. I remember those feelings I had the first time I entered this cave."

"Your first time?" asked Leila. "When was that, and why is this the first time we've seen this cave?"

"I was only three years old when my Papa brought me here when the moon was in Kane," explained Momi. "This is where the Puhi clan renews our mana with the help of our ancestors. You and Hoku are not part of the Puhi clan, so we could not bring you here on our sacred night. Now that you have entered our most sacred place, it has changed that. You are family now, with full access to this place and its secrets."

"Is that why Paul and Martin disappear from the house during the new moon phase?" asked Hoku.

"Ah ha," chuckled Momi. "You've been paying attention. Yes, Kane is night 26 of the moon cycle, just before the moon completely disappears for the new moon. That is our sacred night."

Hoku nodded and glanced at the tall stacks of ki'ai baskets. "It's intimidating to know that each of those baskets contains the bones of a real person," said Hoku. "It's scary, but I love it!"

"Thank you for letting me use this sacred place," said Misty through chattering teeth, "but it's cold here."

"So sorry, my dear," replied Momi as she hugged Misty and rubbed her arms. "Hoku, go to the canoe and get the green duffle bag. Bring it to me, okay, dear?"

Hoku hurried to the canoe, grabbed the large green duffle bag, and took it to Aunty Momi.

"Aunty, you got the whole house in that bag or what?" asked Hoku. "It's so heavy!"

"We never know what we will face when we come here every month, so I try to be prepared," answered Momi as she unzipped the bag.

"Here's some towels to dry off," said Momi. "See the white cord running between the two posts back there? Hang up the towels there when you are done."

While Hoku, Misty, and Leila dried off, Momi retrieved an oversized gray pullover sweater and gave it to Misty. Since Misty had not been among humans for a while, Leila helped Misty put on the garment. The sweater was more like a dress, extending down to Misty's knees.

"So, how's the sweater?" asked Momi.

"I forgot how clothes felt around my body," replied Misty. "This feels wonderful!"

"Very good. I have a spare sweater in the bag just in case you need it."

"Thank you, you are very kind."

"Stay here," said Momi, "while the girls and I set up this place for you, okay? Keep your tail end in the water so the cleaner fish can do their work. Sit on your towel so your bottom doesn't get scraped up by the lava rocks."

"I will," replied Misty, dipping her dolphin tail into the water. Immediately, a swarm of tiny black wrasses clustered around Misty's injury and began nibbling away at the dead tissue clinging to Misty's tail. Misty giggled.

"Are you okay, Mom?" asked Leila.

"That tickles!" replied Misty with a smile on her face.

"I'm glad you are enjoying that," a grinning Momi said as she rummaged through the duffle bag. "Aha! I got them!"

Momi pulled out three colorful pareos, long rectangular sheets of cloth that could be fashioned into sarongs. She tossed one to Leila and another to Hoku, then quickly tied her pareo just above her breast. The girls promptly fashioned their sarongs and waited for Momi's directions.

"Okay, now that we are halfway decent," said Momi, "we can set up a place for Misty to sleep. First, Hoku, you see the eight pipes sticking down from the ceiling of the cave?"

"Yes, Aunty. What are they?"

"That is where we get air into the cave. Put that long piece of bamboo up the pipe to ensure nothing is stuck inside."

"Will do." Hoku grabbed the bamboo and began poking it into one of the pipes. An avalanche of dirt, sand, dried seaweed, and black cockroaches poured through the pipe.

"Ew, that's gross," grumbled Hoku.

"Not even," laughed Momi. "Sometimes, idiots piss down these pipes, not realizing where it goes. Be careful."

"Aunty, you always give me the dirtiest jobs!"

Momi laughed and turned to Leila. "Let's make a bed for your mom near the water so she can easily get to it."

"That would be good. Where do we start?"

Momi pointed to a roll of lauhala (pandanus) mats next to the canoe.

"Go to the roll of mats and remove four mats from the middle. They should be clean. They are sleeping mats in case we get tired and want to spend the night with our ancestors."

"Okay, Aunty."

"When you are done, place them where your mother is sitting. That is the best place to make her bed."

Leila scurried to the roll of mats and unrolled them. Each mat was about 4 feet wide and 8 feet long.

"Aunty, why are these mats so long?"

Momi smiled. "Because the ones that used them were very tall."

"Your ancestors were giants!"

Momi nodded and pointed to the tallest ki'ai propped up against the back of the cave. "You see that basket back there? That is the first eel shapeshifter in our family to settle in Hawaii. In his human form, he was over 8 feet tall."

"Where did he come from? Why did he come to Hawaii?"

"He is from Tahiti. He came here to Hawaii to escape famine and war. When he arrived in Hawaii, he found the people who had settled there were peaceful and generous. They knew nothing about war and had no offensive weapons other than the spears they used for fishing."

"How did the people react to him?"

"They knew he was special because of his size and was quickly given several wives from the prominent families. Ancestor became a famous fisherman, using his shapeshifting abilities to fill his canoe with the best fish of the season. He taught the people how to manage the reef's resources and was the first to suggest restrictions on fishing due to the spawning dates."

"So, he was a fisherman and a teacher?"

"Yes, he was. When he died, his descendants performed a ceremony that made him the family Aumakua, or spirit protector. He watches our back and protects us."

"What is the ancestor's name?"

Momi smiled. "That is an excellent question, but the answer should not be shared outside our bloodline. You are Hanai or adopted into our family, but we do not share the same blood."

"Please excuse me, Aunty. I did not mean to pry."

"No worry, sweetie," said Momi, "No offense taken."

"So, your family are eels. Do you know how the other shapeshifters came to Hawaii? Were they always here?" asked Leila.

Momi paused to consider Leila's question before answering.

"I wonder if the original Hawaiians had shapeshifters. My Papa told me that most shapeshifting clans are from somewhere other than Hawaii. Other shape-shifting families from Tahiti and other parts of Polynesia began to arrive in Hawaii at the same time as our Puhi ancestors. He recognized the newcomers by their language, as it was the language he was fluent in. Ancestor had to learn the Hawaiian language spoken by the natives here since it was quite different from where he came from. Whatever war or famine in the South Pacific occurring during that time must have been awful to force our people to migrate."

Leila glanced toward the back of the cave where feather cloaks, helmets, and spears were displayed.

"Aunty, were some of your ancestors' warriors and chiefs?"

"Yes, they were," replied Momi, "mainly by necessity. Not by choice."

"What do you mean?"

"Eels prefer to observe and avoid conflict. However, mess with us or any of our family, and we'll bite your head off."

"But I thought you said the Hawaiian people were peaceful when Ancestor arrived?"

"Yes, they were, but a few generations later, things changed. New people with new gods and rulers invaded this land. For these foreigners, warfare was a way of life.

Most of the family tried to remain peaceful fishermen. Still, a few of the family chose the warrior's way."

"What became of these warriors?"

Momi laughed. "Have you ever tried to grab an eel with your bare hands?"

"Yeah, when Paul was a baby, I tried. It's almost impossible."

"Well, that is what other warriors discovered when they faced my ancestors in battle. No one could grab them; spears slid off them like raindrops, and they moved like wind through the forest. After proving their worth on the battlefield, many of our warriors were made chiefs and given large tracts of land to manage. The land we are living on was a gift that goes back six generations. Those spears and feather cloaks are just a few of the many my ancestors accumulated over time."

"That was an amazing story, Aunty. Thanks for sharing."

"You are most welcome, my dear," smiled Momi. "Come, let's finish making your mom's bed."

"Aunty, I want to spend more time with my mom until she gets accustomed to the cave. Can we make a bed for me, too?"

"That is why I told you to take out four mats. Two for you and two for your mom. Let's see how your mom is doing."

Misty had fallen asleep while the cleaner fish did their job.

"Let's make your mom's bed right behind her so she can get to it quickly, "said Momi. "Place two mats here for your mom and two more next to it for you."

Misty jolted from her sleep after sensing movement behind her.

"Sorry, Mom!" said Leila. "We were just making your bed."

"We didn't mean to sneak up on you like that," said Momi. "We didn't want to wake you up."

Misty caught her breath and laughed. "It was the first time I slept with my human brain in ten years. I can see that even when I am a human, the dolphin awareness is still there."

"I know what you mean," said Momi. "Those animal instincts never really leave us."

"Still, I forgot how restful it is to have my entire brain shut down. I feel quite refreshed right now."

"Mom, we made a bed for you right next to where you were napping. You can use it when you want or stay in the water. Whatever works better for you will be fine."

"Thanks for that. I will remove this lovely sweater and hang out in the water today. It's more comfortable than dangling what's left of my tail over the edge of the rocks. I'll come up on land tomorrow.

"Yes," said Momi. "The wound needs time to heal. After the cleaner fish are done, the ancestors will use herbs to speed up the healing process. When that happens, you will need to keep the wound dry."

"Mom," said Leila, "I will stay with you until you can manage things yourself."

"Can my pod come and visit me? I have two sons, one that is only three years old, that need my attention."

"Your three-year-old is weaned by now, right?" asked Momi.

"Yes, he is. The other son is six, going to be seven."

"They are welcome to the cove but cannot enter this cave," said Momi. "It would be better to meet your pod in the cove and not mention the cave to them. I know you can hear them when they are near, so meet them outside, ok?"

"I understand." Said Misty. "The pod helps feed me. How will I get enough food in the cave?"

"Don't worry," answered Momi. "The ancestors will make sure you have plenty of fish and squid from the ocean. We will bring you additional food and fresh water. The ancestors will provide everything you need to heal your wounds. Once the herbs are applied to your feet and tail, I will help monitor your progress and provide you with any supplies you may need."

"Thank you, Momi," said Misty.

"You're welcome, sweetie," said Momi. "Leila can check the canoe for any supplies you may need. We have lamps, candles, blankets, extra clothes, and canned goods if needed. Is there anything I can get you?"

"We're good for now!" said Misty.

Momi hugged Misty and Leila. Hoku emerged from the back of the cave.

"There's a lot of cool things in here, Aunty," exclaimed Hoku.

"I know," answered Momi. "And they are here because we don't tell anyone about this place, got it?"

"Oh yeah," replied Hoku. "I can just see how collectors would go nuts with these things."

"Well," interrupted Momi, "Give the ladies a hug, and let's go home."

"See you later, dolphin girl," mumbled Hoku as she hugged Leila. "And you too, dolphin momma."

Momi leaped into the pond and shifted into her eel form. Hoku pounced on Momi's back, and they quickly left the cave.

Alone in the cave, Misty turned to Leila. "Thanks for staying with me and introducing me to this family. They seem to be wonderful people."

"Yes, they are. I love them."

"I can see that," replied Misty. "Aunty Momi treats you like a real daughter."

"That she does, Mom."

"Well, since we are going to spend more time together, is there anything you want to discuss that you've been curious about?

Misty's eyes lit up. "Yes, Mom, I do have something I want to know more about."

"What is it, my girl?"

"Tell me more about my dad."

Chapter 4: Mending Wounds

Shortly after Momi and Hoku left the cave, the tide began to turn, causing the water levels to rise. Suddenly, three long shadows appeared in the pool and moved closer to where Misty rested. The shadows morphed into women as they emerged from the water and climbed to the cave's ledge. Each of the women held a handful of seaweed in their hands.

"Aloha," said the first woman. "My name is Pua, and these are my sisters are Li'i and Makena. We brought some herbs to help heal your tail."

"Thank you, Pua," said Misty. "What do I need to do?"

"Just sit back and relax for now while we combine these herbs and make a poultice," smiled Li'i. "Let's take a look at the wound first."

Misty lifted her tail, and the three sisters examined it for signs of decay and infection.

"The cleaner fish did a fine job of removing the dead tissue, so you are ready for the poultice," said a pleased Makena. "Did Momi leave you some wraps or bandages?"

"Momi left us a medical kit," answered Leila as she scrambled to the canoe and pulled out a white metal box with a red cross painted on the lid. "Here it is."

Pua opened the medical kit and took out a roll of gauze. "Very good," said Pua. "Once we make the poultice, we will place it over the wound and secure it with gauze. You must stay out of the water and keep the dressing dry for three days. Understand?"

"Yes," answered Misty.

"Great. Wait for us here while we prepare the herbs," said Pua.

The three sisters walked to the back of the cave and clustered around a small stone altar. After a short chant, the sisters carefully ground and mixed the seaweed. The cave vibrated with an eerie energy as the poultice was being prepared.

"You feel that?" asked Misty.

"Oh yeah," answered Leila. "It's giving me chicken skin!"

Within a few minutes, Pua returned to Misty with a bowl containing a slimy greenish-red substance.

"Since you will be out of the water for a few days, you should remain human," said Pua. "Please give me your right leg."

Misty raised her right leg, and Pua applied the poultice to the wounded area. With the wound fully coated with the dressing, Li'i and Makena wrapped the wound with gauze. They repeated the process with her left leg.

Misty noticed an immediate difference in how her legs felt as the poultice soothed and coated her wound.

"Oh! That feels so much better," she sighed. Thank you so much."

"You are welcome," replied Pua with a smile. "This poultice will speed your healing and prevent infection if you follow my instructions."

With both feet wrapped, Pua continued instructing Misty about caring for the wound.

"Again, keep your feet out of the water. The poultice will cause a lot of different sensations, especially when you sleep."

"Yes," said Li'i. "It may itch like crazy, but don't scratch it, okay?"

"Also, when you sleep," added Makena, "it may feel like someone is massaging your limbs. This is good. It helps keep the blood circulating so you will heal faster."

"Do you have any questions?"

"Yes," said Leila. "When you and your sisters were mixing the herbs, we felt a strange energy enter the cave. What was that?"

Pua laughed. "We asked other healers in our family to join us, and they did. They chose to stay hidden from you, but their mana is what you felt. It's good that you can sense them. They want to help, so don't be afraid."

"Thanks for explaining that to us," said Misty. "We appreciate your family for what they do for me and welcome their presence."

"Glad to help. We will be back tomorrow to check on you at this time. We realize you are still on dolphin time, which means this is when you should be sleeping,"

"Yes," said Misty. "We were hunting all night, and I am getting tired right now."

"We will let you rest now and see you tomorrow."

The three sisters leaped back into the water and quickly disappeared from the cave as they morphed into their eel form and swam away.

"Mom," said Leila, "Do you need help with your bedding?"

"Not right now, but I may need help relieving myself later."

A large wooden bowl suddenly flew toward Misty and landed with a thud within her reach.

Leila retrieved the bowl and smiled. "Looks like the ancestors want you to use this."

"Considering my choices, this bowl will work just fine. Mahalo ancestors!"

Leila placed the wooden bowl next to Misty and some tissues, then leaned to kiss her mother as she drifted off to sleep.

"Mom, ever since you told me about Chris, my biological father, I've been curious about him."

"I thought I shared much about him last night," replied Misty sleepily.

"You did, but you talked about things you did together, not about who he is. I want to know more about him."

"Baby girl, I was with your father for less than a year, then left him without a word when I got pregnant.

"Yes, I know that. But what is Chris' last name? Was fishing his main job?"

"Baby, I am tired right now. Can we talk about this when I am rested?"

"Sure, but can you give me his last name?"

"Okay, then you promise to let me sleep?"

"Yes, I promise."

"His name is Chris Hardy. Christian Hardy."

"Thank you, Mom."

Leila hugged Misty, and both fell into a deep, restful sleep. After a few hours, Leila sprang up from her bed to check on Misty. Misty was still fast asleep, so Leila quietly slid into the water, shifting into her dolphin form. Once she left the cave, she used her echolocation to track down Victor's boat trolling outside Waialua.

Victor and his brother Harold were hitting a massive school of Aku and did not have clients with them. Leila approached the boat and launched onto the deck with a mighty tail flip.

"Holy shit!" screamed Harold, almost wetting himself. "I thought you were a shark!"

"Not today, Uncle," laughed Leila.

"Um, girl," said Victor, looking away. "Get some clothes on, will you?"

Leila quickly ducked into the lower cabin, slipped on a long-sleeved shirt, a pair of shorts, and boating shoes she left on Victor's boat for emergencies, and rejoined Uncle and Victor on deck.

"So, how is your mom doing?"

"Three ancestors came and made this slimy thing to heal her legs. Mom is sleeping right now, so I'm letting her rest."

"Good," said Victor. "We can use another hand. The fish market is paying good for Aku, so grab a pole, and let's get our share."

"Sure thing, Uncle."

Victor, Harold, and Leila continued to haul fish from the school of Aku until their coolers were filled to the maximum. Victor turned his boat toward Haleiwa, and the heavily laden vessel headed home.

"Hey, Uncle Vic," said Leila. "Do you know who Chris Hardy is?"

Victor and Harold both laughed and nodded their heads. "Oh yeah," answered Victor. "I know him. We all know him. Why do you ask?"

Sensing that Victor and Harold knew more than they would share without prompting, Leila decided she could get more information if she remained nonchalant.

"I just heard the name mentioned and was curious. That's all."

"This guy, Chris," said Harold, "comes from one good family, plenty of money, land, and connections. He could have been anything he wanted to be, but instead, he's one drunk bum and broke-ass fisherman."

"Be nice, brother," scolded Victor. "I heard he's like that because some chick broke his heart. You remember that?"

"Yeah," answered Harold, shaking his head. "Waste time; no woman is worth that!"

Leila glared at Harold. "Perhaps she was his true love! Did any of you even meet this woman?"

"Not really," said Harold. "But we see her every time we pass his house."

"What do you mean?" asked Leila, puzzled.

"Chris turned his heartbreak into art," said Victor. "He has paintings, carvings, and sketches of this woman all over his property. It almost seems like his place is a shrine for her memory."

"What does he do with the art pieces?" asked Leila as she turned to Victor, who seemed more receptive to her questions.

"Some pieces are so beautiful that people pay him big money. The rest of it he keeps around his house. Many wooden sculptures are made from driftwood, milo, monkeypod, and Koa," added Victor.

"So where does he live?"

"He lives in a beach house in Waialua."

"Can you take me to see this man's art collection?"

"Why are you so interested in that?"

"I am just curious. His story is sad and interesting. Makes me want to understand his pain."

"Well, let's get the Aku to the market. Then, if we have time, we'll swing by and see if Chris is out and about."

Leila hugged Victor. "Thank you, Uncle Vic."

Victor finally moored his boat at his slip in Haleiwa boat harbor. Once safely docked, Victor and Harold sorted through the aku, separating the catch by size. The larger, heavier fish brought a better price at the market. In contrast, the smaller ones were taken home, processed, dried, or consumed fresh by friends and family. With the catch sorted and iced, the men loaded four huge coolers onto Harold's truck. The trio then left for the Fish Auction House in Honolulu.

"So, girl," asked Victor. "When do we need to take food to your mom? She may still be on dolphin time, so I'm not sure when we need to take her something to eat."

"Mom should be okay for another four or five hours," replied Leila. "She's human now, so she will be more human than a dolphin."

"It's crazy, you shapeshifters," laughed Harold. "Switching forms must be very confusing."

"Yeah, Uncle Harold," said Leila. "Sometimes we make mistakes and forget where we are. It can upset those who don't know anything about us."

"Oh yeah," laughed Victor. "Remember when I took you to Ali'i Beach when you were still healing from the spear? You were so excited that you were in the ocean again. You began spinning in your dolphin form."

"That freaked out many people, but they tried to catch me once they figured I was a dolphin, not a shark."

"How did you get away from them?" asked Harold.

"Uncle Victor pointed me to the breakwater walls, so I quickly swam to it, then crawled up the stone wall opposite where people were. Luckily, nobody was fishing that day."

"Well, it will be nice to finally meet your mom after these years of taking care of you," said Victor. "Unlike my wife, Momi, I need my boat to survive in the ocean."

"My mom knows who you are and has seen you on your boat several times, especially when I am with you."

"I figured the dolphin pods had something to do with you, not me," laughed Victor.

"Can't be for your good looks," joked Harold.

The playful banter continued until they reached the Fish Market located near the Honolulu waterfront. The market was a large open warehouse packed with trucks, forklifts, and colorful ice chests of varying sizes. Spotting his seller at the Fish Market, Victor waved him down.

"Sonny!" shouted Victor.

A short, stout, older Asian man turned and smiled widely at Victor.

"Hey Victor, what you got for me today?"

"We have four coolers of aku. What can you do for me?"

"Let me see what you got. Good price for aku today."

Victor opened his coolers, revealing his catch.

"Beautiful, fresh catch," grinned Sonny. "I'll take all of it."

"Great. Thanks, Sonny," said Victor happily. Sonny and Victor shook hands, and a team of workers immediately arrived with larger containers. The workers transferred Victor's catch into the containers before whisking the fish to a weighing station.

"Let's get the weight of this catch! Fifteen seventy-five," shouted a man at the weighing station.

"I will put this lot up for sale and get the best price for you," said Sonny. "We will credit your account once we collect."

"Mahalo Sonny," replied Victor. "I trust you will."

Sonny and his workers disappeared into the warehouse with the cache of fish. Victor, Harold, and Leila loaded their empty coolers into the truck and headed toward the North Shore.

"Where to, boss?" teased Harold.

"I need to pick up some parts for my motors," kidded Victor. "Let's stop in Aiea to check out what they have."

"Uncle!" complained Leila, "You guys are terrible. Can you please take me to Chris's place?"

Victor and Harold laughed. "Okay," replied Victor. "Harold, you know how to get there?"

"Yes, brother. I know where it is."

Reaching Haleiwa from Honolulu seemed to take forever for Leila. Her imagination went wild, thinking of the many scenarios that could play out once they got Chris's place. Lost in her thoughts, Leila did not notice that the truck had come to a complete stop.

"Here you go, Leila, "said Harold. "This is the place."

Leila sat up in her seat and glanced outside of the window. She was stunned at what she saw. At the entrance to Chris's property stood a large wood carving of a woman, half dolphin, and half human. The woman's face was finely sculpted, with details and curves that showed love and attention to detail. It was a face Leila knew all too well, for it belonged to her mom, Misty.

Chapter 5: The Shrine

Leila scrambled over Victor and quickly exited the truck to get a closer look at the sculpture of her mom.

"Damn it, girl, what's going on?" demanded Victor as he and Harold exited the truck.

His question fell on deaf ears as Leila fixated on the sculpture. She then gazed past the front entrance and observed several more miniature sculptures of Misty placed strategically across Chris's front lawn. The pieces were displayed thoughtfully and reverently. Each sculpture and carving seemed to come alive from its carefully chosen spot. The front yard was immaculately landscaped as if allowing a single weed to sprout was a criminal offense. Leila was speechless as the magnitude of what she saw hit her. Chris still loved her mom! His feelings were evident in each lovingly carved piece. Her heart pounded, realizing that this man never stopped caring for her mother.

"What would he do if he saw her now? What will he say if he discovers who I am?" Leila wondered.

"I told you," said Harold. "This guy is obsessed. Brother, do you think Chris met a shapeshifter and fell in love with her? This place feels like a shrine."

Victor gazed thoughtfully at Leila, then back to Harold. "I think this obsession goes further than that, don't you think Leila?"

Leila bowed her head to avoid eye contact.

"Leila," said Victor, "I know that look when you are trying to hide something. I know you recognize the woman in the sculpture. Who is she?"

Leila's heart began to race. She wasn't sure she wanted her secret revealed just yet.

"Leila!" Victor urged. "Tell us who this woman is."

Leila blew out the breath she didn't know she was holding in.

"She's my mom, Uncle Vic. Chris has been carving my mom."

Victor and Harold stared at Leila in surprise.

"So, your mom is the woman Chris is hung up on? That's crazy!"

"Actually," added Leila, "It's a little crazier than that."

Victor and Harold studied Leila with a perplexed look. What else was Leila hiding?

"What do you mean?" asked Victor.

"Well," Leila paused. "My mom told me that Chris is my dad."

"No way," gasped Harold. "Chris Hardy is your Papa? That is insane!"

The trio studied the house as they absorbed Leila's startling revelation. Chris' house was a typical beach home, a small, weather-worn cottage with peeling green paint.

Suddenly, a tall, slender hapa-haole man appeared on the home's front porch. The man had long, wavy, sun-bleached hair with vivid blue eyes and two weeks of facial hair. He wore a white paint-spattered T-shirt and an old pair of board shorts that had seen better days. His unkempt appearance contrasted greatly with the warm and friendly greeting they received.

"How's it going, folks? Are you guys interested in the sculptures, or are you looking for paintings?"

Panic overcame Leila, causing her to dash for cover in the pickup truck.

"Hi Chris, it's me, Victor, and my brother Harold."

Chris's smile widened as he recognized Victor and Harold.

"Eh, how's the fishing Victor? Long time no see, man. And I remember you, Harold. You're my brother Dennis's classmate. Come inside, have a beer with me."

"Nah, thanks for the offer," said Victor.

"We are heading out after this. Momi is waiting for us to get home."

"Yeah, okay. Some other time then," said Chris.

"So, what can I do for you guys?"

"My Hanai daughter, Leila, asked to see your artwork, so I brought her to see you."

"Oh, that's cool," said Chris, "Where is she?"

"She's hiding in my truck, but she likes your sculptures. She is the reason we stopped by. Leila, come over here and meet Chris."

After a few seconds, the truck door opened, and Leila shyly stepped out. At first glance, Chris could not believe his eyes. With every step Leila took toward him, he became increasingly entranced. His heart was beating wildly, and he found it hard to breathe. Was he seeing things? Chris' unbelieving eyes fixated on Leila as he stared slack-jawed at her.

"M... Misty? Is that you?" he stammered as Leila reached him.

"No, Chris. I am Leila. "Misty is my mom," Leila replied softly.

Shock registered on Chris' face as he processed Leila's words.

"*Misty is my mom.*"

A million thoughts flashed through his head simultaneously, but one question pushed itself to the forefront of his stunned mind.

"Are you a, ah...."

"Shapeshifter? Yes, I am."

Chris' emotions overtook him as he fought to hold back the flood of tears threatening to fall. Never in his mind had he ever dreamed of meeting Misty's child. Yet here she stood, looking like a mirror image of the woman he loved. Hugging her daughter was the next best thing if he couldn't hold Misty.

"Can I hug you, please?" Chris managed to ask in a strangled voice.

"I would love that, Chris," Leila replied.

Victor and Harold turned away to give Chris and Leila privacy and to preserve their manly image.

"Allergy acting up, brother Vic?" teased Harold.

"Shut up, you donkey."

Chris and Leila were frozen in time. For Leila, she finally got to meet and hug her father. She struggled to keep that fact from Chris despite bursting with the moment's excitement.

It was comforting but overwhelming for Chris to have Misty's child in his arms. Even though he was unaware that Leila was his daughter, the fact she was Misty's daughter and Leila's similarity to Misty made Chris feel like he was holding the love of his life in his arms again. Overcome with emotion, Chris's knees gave way, and he crumbled.

"Chris!" shouted Leila as she tried unsuccessfully to hold him up. Victor and Harold responded and attempted to lift Chris from the ground.

"I'm okay," said Chris, "Let me sit here and collect my thoughts for a few minutes. I am just filled with emotions right now. Leila, you look so much like your mother; it's messing with my brain."

"I'm so sorry," said Leila. "I should have found a better way to introduce myself to you."

Chris laughed. "I tell you, that would be a mean trick if you could swing it."

After a few minutes, Chris slowly got to his feet and ran his fingers through his long-matted hair.

"Come in the back and kick back for a bit. You guys have some time?"

"We have to get home by noon," said Victor, "But we have about an hour we can spare for a visit."

"Good. Good. I really want to spend more time with you all."

Chris dodged tools, wood piles, broken cars, and discarded appliances as they walked toward the backyard.

"Looks like we have a pack rat here," whispered Harold to Victor.

"Kinda reminds me of your place, doesn't it, brother?" Victor teased.

Once in the backyard, the three guests noticed a gigantic Kamane tree with large round leaves spreading its branches across most of the backyard. Chris had placed a large round table with eight chairs around it under the shady branches. Near the table, he had dug a barbeque pit in the ground. Unlike the immaculately landscaped front yard, the backyard was left to nature. Chris mowed the lush green lawn, but the foliage springing up along the perimeter was an offering from nature.

"Here," said Chris. "Have a seat. Let me run in the house and grab some drinks."

"Can I help you?" asked Leila.

"Sure! Why not? Come with me."

Chris smiled warmly as he led the way to his kitchen. He still couldn't believe Misty's daughter was here at his home.

Victor and Harold sat at the table and watched Chris and Leila enter the home.

"Looks like they are getting along," smiled Harold.

"Seems like it," replied Victor. "How will he react when he finds Leila is his daughter?"

"I'm not sure. I would not break the news to him today. He might stroke out on us. It's obvious how much meeting Leila has shaken him."

"Well, it's not our place to say anything about that anyway. That is up to Leila and Misty."

Chris and Leila entered the back of the house, which led to the kitchen. A distinct chemical odor masked the trash overflowing the garbage bin.

"What is that chemical smell?" said Leila, trying to be polite.

"Oh, that's from the oil paints I am testing out," said Chris. "The rest is garbage. The maid quit last week," he chuckled.

Leila laughed at Chris' joke. He was not big on cleaning.

"What are you testing the oil paints on, Chris?"

"Well, you saw the carvings outside, right? Somehow, the wood and the stains don't do justice to your mom's beauty, so I've been trying to paint her to bring her to life on canvas. I want everyone to see her as I remember her."

"Now that is cool. Can I see one of your paintings of Mom?"

"Sure. I have one in my studio. It's this way."

Chris guided Leila down a hall leading to a large 20'X 30' air-conditioned room filled with canvas' and easels. Chris flipped on a light that illuminated a covered canvas.

"Here it is," Chris said as he carefully removed the cloth from his painting.

Leila was stunned. The colors, texturing, and composition replicating Misty's image were accurate and authentic. She wondered how Chris could remember every detail after all these years.

"Oh my God! The painting is beautiful! It looks exactly like Mom."

"This is the best one so far," said Chris. "I don't know why, but people are snatching my smaller paintings of her at the different beaches along the North Shore. I've sold hundreds of them."

"If they are anything like this painting, I can see why people like them. It is filled with life, colors, and motion like you are in the painting with her."

"That is what I tried to capture."

"I still can't believe you remember Mom's face in such detail after all these years," exclaimed Leila.

"Well, I have a photographic memory and recall every detail of her face and form," Chris answered.

"That is amazing! You're the only person I know who has that gift. Thank you for sharing this with me, Chris."

Leila hugged Chris, and both wept without shame.

"Leila," said Chris. "Is there any chance that I will see your mom again? There are so many questions I must ask her, and I am willing to do anything to see her one more time so I can get some closure. Do you know where she is? What happened to her? Why did she disappear so suddenly without warning or saying goodbye? She broke my heart when she swam away and never returned. After all this time, I still love her deeply. She was the love of my life, and I need to know why she decided to disappear. Did I do something to make her leave me? I have so many questions that drive me crazy sometimes."

Leila was not prepared to answer any of Chris's questions. "I don't know what happened, Chris. That was before I was born. I know my mom has changed, and some of the changes she experienced may affect how you feel about her."

"What happened to your mom?" asked Chris. "What kind of changes? Is it serious?"

"All I can say is my mom is different from the last time you saw her."

"Can you take me to her? I want to help."

"I know your heart is in the right place. I can see it. Let me talk to my mother and see what she says."

"No matter what happened to your mom, I will do everything I can to help her. Please tell her that."

"I will," promised Leila as she hugged Chris again.

"Okay, what kind of drinks do you, Victor, and Harold like?"

"Cold water should do, or maybe some Pepsi."

"I don't have bottled water, but I do have Pepsi."

Chris opened his refrigerator, retrieved three bottles of Pepsi and a bottle of Heineken beer, and led Leila back to Victor and Harold.

"Thanks for the drinks," said Victor, guzzling half a bottle in one breath. "That hits the spot."

"Yes, thanks so much," said Harold.

"My pleasure," said Chris. "I don't get many visitors, but having Misty's daughter visiting me is a treat."

"Well, thank you, Chris," said Leila softly.

Victor glanced toward the ocean and saw a worn 16-foot flat-bottom boat and fishing nets hung out to dry. Several outboard motors, coolers, and fishing gear were beside a small shack at the beach's edge and Chris' property.

"When did you last take your boat out, Chris?"

"I can't remember, to tell you the truth," sighed Chris.

"I lost interest in the ocean after Misty disappeared. After months of going out hoping to find her, I couldn't take the heartache any longer. Every fishing trip reminded me of what I had lost – the pain of losing her cut like a knife. At first, I drowned my pain in a bottle, but then I began to sculpt and paint her. In a way, it brought her closer to me and helped ease my heartache. Creating my mermaid art is therapy and a tribute to the one woman my heart can never stop loving. My art keeps me sane."

Chris' eyes misted as he stared out toward the ocean sadly. His pain was tangible and touched the hearts of everyone there.

After a minute of silence and reflection, Victor gently changed the subject.

"Your nets are falling apart. When was the last time you started the engines?"

"I don't know, and I don't really care," Chris said, taking a quick swig from this beer bottle. "As I said, I lost interest."

Victor nodded. "How much do you want for the boat?"

"What? You wanna buy my boat?"

"I want to save your boat. It would be a good project for my boys and our Hanai children to refinish the boat and use it in the stream next to our house to catch crabs. So, what do you say?"

"Victor, I don't need your money. If you can tow the boat away, it's yours."

"Really?" said Harold. "Who doesn't need money?"

Chris laughed. "No, really, I am fine. My dad changed his mind about me just before he died and left me and my brother as multi-millionaires. Dad created a trust to manage his assets, so my brother and I don't have to worry about money."

"What happened to your family home in Pupukea? The huge one?" asked Harold.

"We still own it but keep it open for friends and family. It's a monster to keep up. This place here is more my speed."

"You're a multi-millionaire, and yet you choose to live in this small house?" asked Leila.

"I was a multi-millionaire. Now I have enough money to live anywhere and do anything I please. I am here by choice. I love the ocean even if I don't go out on the water nowadays. I don't know. Maybe subconsciously, I am still hoping Misty will return here to me. This is the last place we were together," he trailed off.

"Then what do you do with all your money?" asked Leila.

Victor gave Leila stern looks for asking personal questions to someone she just met.

Leila suddenly realized she was rude, but Chris didn't mind her questions.

"You mean, do I give money away and help needy people? I do what I can, when I can, to people and projects that are worthy. I don't believe in giving people handouts, though. People must prove they deserve the money."

"That's fair," Victor said, pointing to his watch.

"Well, Chris. Thanks for having us, but we need to get moving. It was great seeing you again."

Chris stood and hugged Victor. "Thanks for bringing Leila to see me. I hope that she will be able to convince her mom to see me soon."

"I think that would be good, Chris," smiled Victor.

Leila wrapped her arms tightly around Chris and kissed him on his cheek. Now that she had found her dad, she didn't want to leave him.

"I am so happy to meet you, Chris. I promise I will talk to my mom about you, and we'll see what happens from there."

"That sounds great," said Chris. "And if you need anything, you know where I live, and I am here for you, okay? Please feel free to visit me any time, Leila. My door is always open for you."

"Thank you, Chris," replied Leila softly as she smiled and drank in his image one last time before walking to the truck.

Victor, Harold, and Leila climbed into the vehicle and slowly drove away as Chris watched the truck disappear. What a day it had been.

"Leila," asked Victor. "Did you tell Chris that he is your father?"

"No, I didn't," said Leila. "I wanted to feel him out as a person first."

"What do you think about him now?"

"I like him a lot but feel sorry for him too. He is heartbroken and maybe even bitter because of how Mom left him. I don't blame him. He doesn't know my mom left him because she was pregnant with me. I sometimes wonder why Mom felt she had to run and hide her pregnancy from him. I know she loved him as much as he loved her. Maybe she didn't want him to think she trapped him. It's sad because we have all suffered and lost something precious."

"Yes, choices have consequences, unfortunate for some, a blessing for others," reflected Harold.

"I, for one, am hoping Mom will see Chris, and he will love and accept her despite what happened to her tail."

"We can all hope for a happy ending, Baby girl," replied Victor.

"Well, let's get home and see what Aunty Momi has for your mom's afternoon meal. You can tell your mom about your visit with Chris and see what she says. It would be great if they could reunite happily."

"I think so too. I'm a sucker for true love," agreed Harold.

Victor rolled his eyes and glanced at his brother.

"Whatever you say, man. I just want this to have a happy ending for everyone. It would be great for Leila to have a dad."

Leila sat quietly in the back seat of Victor's truck, quietly agreeing with her Uncle Vic. She said a prayer that not only would Chris love and accept Misty but that he would love and accept his daughter, too.

"Please, God," whispered Leila. "Please let my dad love me."

(STORY CONTINUES IN BOOK III: TAMING THE SHARK)

About The Author

D J Wallace is an author, clairvoyant, reiki master, ha ki'i master, professional remote viewer, healer, ordained minister, life coach, tarot reader, and Native Hawaiian cultural practitioner. He is a retired educator with advanced degrees in Public Administration, Psychology, and Divinity. For more information about D J Wallace, call (808) 349-4788 or visit his website, intuitiveinsightshawaii.com.

OTHER BOOKS BY DJ WALLACE ON AMAZON

Anna Blaze Telepath & Rift Jumper Series

Shark Man of Haleiwa (Kindle Vella)

Angels & Ghosts of Shingles Hospital

There's A Ghost in My House

The Journey of Our Souls: What You Can Learn from One Man's Multiple Near-Death Experiences.

TAROT READING

FEELING LOST AND UNSURE ABOUT YOUR FUTURE?

A DETAILED TAROT READING CAN HELP.

Get an in-depth intuitive tarot reading from DJ
Wallace, a gifted clairvoyant, tarot reader and
remote viewer. Call (808) 349-4788 or visit our store
at www.intuitiveinsightshawaii.com to book your
session.

Made in the USA
Columbia, SC
16 April 2024